after
SHOCK

" I could hear screaming now above the roar, as people realised the deadly danger. The tsunami began lifting people and objects high, tossing them about like rubbish.

It couldn't be happening. These things only happen in disaster movies. But the truth slammed into me with enough power to take my breath away. I was going to drown. "

More great reads in the SHADES 2.0 series:

Witness by Anne Cassidy
Shouting at the Stars by David Belbin
Blitz by David Orme
Virus by Mary Chapman
Fighting Back by Helen Orme
Hunter's Moon by John Townsend
Animal Lab by Malcolm Rose
Tears of a Friend by Jo Cotterill
Danger Money by Mary Chapman
A Murder of Crows by Penny Bates
Doing the Double by Alan Durant
Mantrap by Tish Farrell
Coming in to Land by Dennis Hamley
Life of the Party by Gillian Philip
Plague by David Orme
Treachery by Night by Ann Ruffell
Mind's Eye by Gillian Philip
Gateway from Hell by David Orme
Four Degrees More by Malcolm Rose
Who Cares? by Helen Orme
Cry, Baby by Jill Atkins
The Messenger by John Townsend
Asteroid by Malcolm Rose
Space Explorers by David Orme
Hauntings by Mary Chapman
The Scream by Penny Bates
Rising Tide by Anne Rooney
Stone Robbers by Tish Farrell
Fire! by David Orme
Invasion by Mary Chapman
What About Me? by Helen Orme
Flood by David Orme
The Real Test by Jill Atkins
Mau Mau Brother by Tish Farrell
Sixteen Bricks Down by Dennis Hamley
Crying Out by Clare Lawrence
Gunshots at Dawn by Mary Chapman
The Calling by Penny Bates
Ben's Room by Barbara Catchpole
The Phoenix Conspiracy by Mary Chapman
The Team with the Ghost Player by Dennis Hamley
Death on Toast by John Townsend
Flashback by John Townsend
No Good by Helen Orme

after SHOCK

Jill Atkins

Ransom

SHADES 2.0
Aftershock
by Jill Atkins

Published by Ransom Publishing Ltd.
Radley House, 8 St. Cross Road, Winchester, Hampshire SO23 9HX, UK
www.ransom.co.uk

ISBN   978 178127 629 7
First published in 2014

CONTENTS

One 7

Two 16

Three 23

Four 33

Five 43

Six 51

I can't remember how the row started. Me
and Mum, as usual. Probably some stupid
little thing, I expect. Not really important,
just seemed it at the time. We were in the
living room of the wooden bungalow,
standing facing each other like female
wrestlers in the ring.

Dad was sitting in the corner reading,

ignoring us. He was used to us rowing. We did it all the time.

'And another thing ... ' Mum always said that, giving herself time to invent the next complaint. She really knew how to wind me up, big time. She pointed at me. 'Your bikini is much too revealing ... If I'd gone with you when you bought it ... '

'Get real, Mother!'

' ... And you're wearing too much make-up.'

I clenched my fists, but kept them by my sides to stop myself hitting out at her.

'You're pathetic!' I yelled. 'Get into the twenty-first century, will you? All my friends wear loads more make-up than me.'

'Yes, and just look at them,' Mum ranted on. 'I won't have you getting yourself into trouble like them ... '

I broke away and stormed towards the

door. Dad looked up from his book.

'So, a couple of my friends have been in trouble with the police and Suki has got herself pregnant, but ... '

'That's exactly what I'm getting at ... I won't let you ... '

'Let me? *Let me?*' I yelled. 'What are you, my owner?'

'I'm your mother, for God's sake ... '

'I'm going out,' I shouted. 'What a holiday! I thought it would be great, coming to a place like this ... the most beautiful place on Earth, it's supposed to be. Well I'm going to find a bit of peace and quiet on the beach.'

'No!' Mum shouted, darting after me and gripping my arm. 'You can't. Not now. I promised Babs and Tony we'd go across to their bungalow in a few minutes.'

'Don't touch me!' I shook off her hand.

'You can go to boring Babs and tiresome Tony's bungalow if you like,' I snapped as I opened the door. 'But I'm not going.'

'Don't be so selfish,' hissed Mum.

'Me? Selfish?' My head was about to explode. 'Why should I be forced to go? They're not *my* so-called friends. They're a couple of middle-aged losers. Anyway, Damian doesn't have to go, does he? I heard him go out early. I suppose he's scuba-diving with those two guys he met the other day.'

'That's different … he's a lot older than you.'

'That's no reason. He's always been your favourite … '

'Madeleine!'

That did it! I'm Maddy! I can't bear being called Madeleine and she knows that. She only uses it when she really wants to annoy me.

'I hate you!' I yelled, as I shoved open the door. 'And I know you hate me. You wouldn't even care if you never saw me again.'

'Maddy … !' I heard Dad call as I ran out into the sunshine, but I couldn't be bothered to listen to him. He's more reasonable than Mum, but I didn't expect him to defend me. He'd more likely ask me to apologise. And that I wasn't willing to do!

I snatched a towel from the rail on the veranda and ran out of the little complex of bungalows, across the grass and through the grove of palm trees. I passed the local people selling fish and beach mats and fruit and touristy stuff, ignoring their greetings and smiles.

I didn't stop until I arrived at the beach

and I felt the hot, soft sand sifting up between my toes.

Breathing heavily, with both anger and the speed of my running, I walked for a few metres then sank down onto my towel, well away from everyone else.

I didn't feel at all sociable, not after that session with Mum. I needed to forget her and enjoy myself, get myself a decent all-over (well, almost all-over) tan and go home in ten days' time to be the envy of my friends.

I stared out to sea, feeling my breathing slow down and my body relax, as the gentle waves tumbled onto the beach fifty metres away.

I could see the brightly coloured sails of windsurfers and three small yachts bobbing about on the calm water, as they tacked from side to side.

A motorboat shot across the bay. I watched the water-skier following in its wake, until he turned a somersault and toppled into the water.

People sunbathed. Children paddled and splashed. I could hear their distant chatter and laughter as they played in the sand and chased each other in the shallow water.

I wondered where Damian was. Somewhere out there amongst the coral, I supposed, lucky beggar. I had hardly seen him since we arrived on the island. He'd spent more time under water than on land. I wished I could be scuba-diving with him.

Putting thoughts of my brother aside, I turned and looked up at the palm trees behind me and watched the thin, feathery branches dancing lightly in the breeze. I could just see the bungalows in the distance.

This was more like it. Paradise!

I lay back, feeling the warmth of the sand and the heat of the sun on my face. Totally relaxed now, I closed my eyes and listened. I love that sound of the sea, especially the hiss as the waves are drawn back across the sand.

I don't know if I dozed off, or how long I had been lying there, but suddenly I was wide awake. Instinctively, I knew something wasn't right.

I lay for a moment staring up at the bright blue sky. What was wrong?

Then I knew. The sound of the sea. The rush and hiss had stopped. There was an eerie silence.

I sat up, feeling my heart racing, though I couldn't make out why I felt so frightened. But when I looked towards the sea, I gasped and leapt to my feet. Instead of the shallows and calm water beyond, there was a never-ending stretch of flat sand.

The sea had disappeared!

TWO

I screamed. I couldn't help myself.
I couldn't understand what was happening.
It somehow felt like I had landed in the
middle of a horror movie. A few people
stared at me, but all I could do then was
point.

I pointed down the long, extended beach
that stretched as far as I could see. It wasn't

like the tide going out. It was much, much more sinister, as if the sea had been sucked away.

Where had it gone? It couldn't just have vanished. Seas don't do that. Do they?

I screamed again. I could see fish flapping helplessly on the wet sand, where only a few minutes ago they had been swimming. Men and women and children stood motionless where they had been messing about in the sea.

And what had happened to the windsurfers and the people in their boats? They had gone, too!

At that moment, my stomach lurched violently. I forgot the row with Mum. I just wanted to be with her and Dad. I had to get back to the bungalow.

I tried to run, but the dry sand was deep and I felt I was running in sticky treacle.

My legs were weak and limp like a rag doll's, but at last I reached the top of the beach.

I don't know what made me turn at that moment. I guess it must have been the distant roar that had begun to resound in my ears. What I saw then froze me rigid for several seconds. I wanted to warn everyone around me, and those people running towards the sea, gathering the fish – an easy catch, a free lunch.

But I couldn't move.

There was a wall of water, a giant wall, way out in the distance for the moment, but heading my way, fast.

The roar grew louder. The wall was moving in. Managing to force my legs to work, I ran, panic bubbling over inside me. We had been studying natural disasters at school last term and I had suddenly recognised what I was seeing – the sucking back of the sea, the massive wall of water.

It was a tsunami! A gigantic wave that rushes in from the ocean, destroying all before it. I couldn't quite remember where it had come from or how it was formed, but all I knew was that it was coming for me. To destroy me!

'Mum!' I screamed, as my fear gave me strength and made me run faster than ever before.

'Dad! The sea! It's coming. Get out, up, away!'

The bungalows were just ahead. I recognised ours; the towels on the veranda. The door was shut.

'Mum, Dad!' I yelled, as I dashed up to the wooden door and forced it open. But they were not there. They must be at Babs and Tony's. I couldn't remember which one that was. Anyway, there was no time.

The roar was almost deafening. The wall of water was still coming, building itself higher and higher, stronger and stronger, as it came nearer and nearer.

I couldn't believe it. There were people standing facing the sea, filming it. They didn't realise what it was. I could imagine they were planning to show this off to their neighbours when they got home: 'Look what we saw – isn't it fantastic?'

'Get away!' I yelled. 'It's a tsunami!'

But I found that even I stood spellbound in the doorway for a few seconds. I couldn't take my eyes off that massive force of water hurtling towards me, up the beach and into the trees.

I could hear screaming and shouting now above the roar, as more and more people realised its deadly danger. It began lifting people and objects high and tossing them about like rubbish. It was smashing everything in its path.

I tried to reassure myself. It wasn't real. It couldn't be happening. These things only happen in disaster movies.

But the truth slammed into me with enough power to take my breath away. It was going to lift me and hurl me like an unwanted toy. I was going to drown.

I didn't want to die.

Mum and Dad were somewhere near, in one of the bungalows. Had they heard it yet? Did they know a wall of water was about to wash them away? Were they as terrified as I was?

And Damian! Where was he now? Scuba-diving. In the worst place to be – the sea. The sea that had disappeared, then turned into a wild ferocious animal.

Please, let them be all right.

I held my hands over my ears to try and cut out some of the roar that was louder than the noisiest thunderclap I had ever heard.

The light had faded with the shadow of the looming wave. What could I do? I had no choice. Rushing into the bungalow, I slammed the door, wondering if the wooden structure would stand up to that mighty force.

I only had seconds to find out.

THREE

Everything went black. The whole building shuddered as the first wave struck. There was a loud crack. I guessed it was the window smashing or the door being forced open.

I instinctively tensed my body as I was thrown backwards, crashing painfully against the far wall of the bungalow as the wave burst in.

The water was freezing! The cold took my breath away. Then I gasped and found myself swallowing water. I remember the foul salty taste as it surged up my nose and down my throat.

All the time, I was struggling, trying to lift my head above the surface, frantically kicking my legs and pulling with all the strength of my arms. I was panicking, fighting for my life.

A moment later, the water became calmer for a few seconds. I managed to come up for air, coughing and choking and spitting out the evil-tasting liquid. As my eyes got used to the semi-darkness, I could see I was out of my depth in churning, murky water.

The bungalow had survived the wave. I trod water, shivering, searching for something to hang on to.

Spotting a wooden table bobbing about on the water on the other side of the room, I swam across and grabbed hold of it. It made me feel just a little bit safer.

But then I almost freaked out. My head was almost up to the ceiling and the water was rising.

If it rose much further, I would run out of air and I would drown. Then something told me that if I went outside, at least I might stand a chance.

But before I could make a move, there was the loudest rumble ever, as if the whole world outside had exploded. I braced myself for a second time as an even stronger wave crashed violently against the bungalow. The whole building juddered. Then it was ripped open like balsa wood.

I was washed out, up ... I had no idea

where. Totally helpless, I closed my eyes, held my breath and clung desperately to the table.

At first, it seemed like I was spinning in a whirlpool, round and round, very fast. I felt dizzy and sick. I just wished it would stop.

Soon the whirlpool became a flood and I was swept along in it, travelling at terrifying speed. Realising that the table had brought me to the surface, I gasped in air and dared to open my eyes.

What a horrible sight. The water was littered with dead fish, branches, planks of wood, a shoe, a beach mat, a child's toy, a sunshade ...

Everything swirled around me as I was carried along further and further away from the sea.

Something bumped hard against me. Ugh! I almost let go of the table. It was a man's body. He was dressed in red bathing trunks and I could tell he was dead. His eyes were staring, but I knew he couldn't see.

I had never seen a dead body before, except in movies. I didn't ever want to see another one, but soon realised there were others in the flood around me.

I trembled all over. My arms felt so weak I was in danger of losing my grip, but I had to grit my teeth and hang on.

Then, all of a sudden, the icy water began pulling me and my table down. I held my breath and squeezed my eyes tightly closed. Would I ever come back to the surface? Was I going to drown?

Just as my lungs were about to explode, my head bobbed up out of the water again.

'You're still alive,' I kept saying inside my head. 'Just hold on!' But another part of my brain cried out, 'Mum! Dad! Damian! Where are you?'

I had no idea how long I had been in the water. It was all happening so quickly and yet it seemed like it would never end. It was like a long nightmare where you never woke up. I felt weak and sick and cold and very, very frightened.

But at last, the pace began to slow down. The water was losing its force. The wave was breaking, almost like it was crashing onto a beach. Only now it was on a rocky hillside a long way from the beach.

I let go of my table and the wave threw me forward. Hitting the ground hard, I rolled over and over, until I collided with a rock. I lay still, not daring to move.

After a while, I forced myself to sit up. The

water had gone. Already the land was drying in the heat of the sun. Staring back down the way I had come, I could not believe what I saw.

That calm, beautiful paradise of a short while ago had been smashed, totally destroyed. Scattered across the wide space there were piles of smashed wood, uprooted trees, upside-down cars, plastic chairs, even fishing boats sitting high and dry a long way from the sea.

But the worst thing was the dead bodies! There were so many of them, washed up like driftwood after a storm, lifeless, horrible!

I turned away to try to shut out what I had seen, but the vision would not go away. I was sure I would never ever be able to forget.

The air stank of seaweed and a ghastly

stench I could not identify. I retched and was violently sick.

Looking up the hill behind me, I decided I should go up there, in case the sea came again. Shaking all over and fighting back the tears, I suddenly felt terribly alone.

Where was my family?

I refused to accept that Damian might be dead. And I needed to start searching for Mum and Dad.

Although I felt bruised and battered, I made myself stand up. That was when I realised my left arm was throbbing. I had felt so numb I had not noticed it before. It was hanging limply by my side.

I tried to support it with my right hand as I began to limp on very wobbly legs up the hill.

As I climbed higher, I began to hear voices behind me and I realised with relief that I wasn't the only person to have survived the tsunami. I heard a man's voice yelling names over and over again, and a child screaming.

A woman's crying sent shivers up my spine. Many people were calling, shouting, crying, screaming. They all sounded as desperate as I felt, but although I opened my mouth to call, no sound came out.

To my right, in the distance, I caught sight of a group of people. They were climbing, too.

I looked eagerly for my family, but there was no sign of them. Perhaps they were ahead of me.

That thought made me struggle on, but I had almost reached the top of the hill when the last bit of energy drained away. My legs gave way under me. I collapsed in a heap.

Mum, Dad, Damian ... Where are you?

Unable to keep a grip any longer, I curled up on the ground and sobbed.

FOUR

Eventually, my tears dried up. I had been crying so long, there was nothing left. I felt like a zombie, stiff, brainless, unable to think. I couldn't move, didn't know what to do.

There was a searing pain in my arm, but otherwise I didn't feel anything at all.

'Are you all right?'

I looked up, startled. A grey-haired man stood a few metres away, looking down at me. I hadn't heard him come. He was wearing striped shorts and was covered with streaks of mud. A trickle of blood ran down one side of his face.

'Are you all right?' he asked again.

I shrugged then stared back out towards the sea. It was shining, sparkling with the brilliance of the sun.

A shiver of anger shot through me. How could it be so bright when everything else was brown and dismal and grey? How could it look so calm and innocent after such violence and destruction?

'I'm James,' the man said. 'What's your name?'

'Madeleine,' I managed to whisper. 'Madeleine.'

Hearing myself repeat the name gave me a sharp shock. Suddenly, I had a flash of memory. I was in a wooden bungalow. I was yelling at Mum. Madeleine. That was what Mum had called me. That was why I had said I hated her and run to the beach.

'I wish I hadn't said that to her,' I cried.

It all flooded over me; the water, the waves, Damian in the sea, Mum and Dad at Babs and Tony's ... my fight to survive.

'Mum! Dad! Damian?' I screamed. 'Where are you?'

It hit me in the chest with even more force than that wall of water. Were they all dead?

I screamed again. 'No!'

I leapt to my feet, almost fainting with the pain in my arm, and stared around me. Rushing down the hill, I began madly rummaging amongst the piles of rubble, frantically lifting planks, sunbeds, towels, tree branches.

Uncovering bodies, I rolled them over with my good arm while the other one throbbed unbearably.

There were so many bodies, hundreds, maybe thousands of them, men and women and children, even some tiny babies. All dead!

I rushed from one to another, pulling them, half lifting them, searching.

The man had followed me.

'You need to get to a hospital,' he said. 'That arm looks nasty.'

I shook my head. I had more important things to do. I had to find them.

'My wife, Cathy, and I will take you,' he said.

I glared at this total stranger, wishing he would go away and leave me in peace. I had to find my family.

'I can't,' I yelled at him, anger flaring again inside me. 'Don't you understand? I've got to find them.'

He didn't react, just stood there, watching me. I tried to block him out.

I moved on. I could not stop: lifting, turning over the bodies, searching for familiar faces, yet praying I wouldn't find them.

'Cathy and I both need patching up,' he went on. 'I've got a gash on my head and she's got cuts and bruises. We were extremely lucky.'

'Go away!' I yelled.

But he was still there.

I began to think. Who was he, anyway? I'd never met him before. Why was he taking such an interest in me? And where was this wife, Cathy? Had he made her up to try to take advantage of me?

'There must have been a massive earthquake somewhere across the ocean,' he said. 'To cause a wave that big.'

Of course, now I remembered that lesson in school. It hadn't really meant anything to me at the time. It did now!

'Cathy and I have been on this island for quite a few months,' James said. 'So we know the region. There's a hospital about a mile … '

'Can't you take no for an answer?'

'Look, there's a fair chance your parents are OK,' he said. 'We'll just as likely find them at the hospital. They'll be searching for you. They'll be as worried about you as you are about them.'

I guess it was those words that made me start to change my mind. Maybe I had to trust him. Maybe he was right. Maybe Mum and Dad had been washed up alive like me, further along the hill.

Anyway, I couldn't carry on with what I was doing. It was so revolting and I had begun to feel sick again.

I'd never even seen one dead body in my life before, and now there were thousands of them. And I'd been touching them. I knew I'd have nightmares about them for the rest of my life.

At that moment, I noticed a small, white-haired woman limping towards us. She was dressed in shorts and T-shirt, and I could see blood through the mud on her arms and legs.

'This is Cathy,' said James.

'Hello,' she said. 'Come on, James. Let's get to that hospital.'

I made the decision. I would go with them. It would be better than being alone. The hospital would be a good place to look.

My parents might be there.

James nodded. 'All right, dear. Coming, Madeleine?'

'OK,' I muttered. 'Thanks.' Before this happened I would have told them to call me Maddy, but now I realised how unimportant that was.

We walked for ages, away from the sea, with the sun climbing higher and higher in the sky. It grew hotter and hotter. I was desperate for a drink, but everywhere was totally dry. Several times, I collapsed to the ground. My legs ached so much and the throbbing in my arm was much worse. I wanted to give up. But James and Cathy managed to persuade me to keep going.

'Only a little bit further,' Cathy kept saying, taking my good arm. 'We're almost there.'

As we walked, we met children looking for parents and parents looking for children. Most of them were tearful. All of them looked desperate.

Everyone was frantically searching for someone else. Some were on holiday like me, but I realised after a while that for many people this was their home. Their country had been flattened and devastated by the tsunami.

We were all heading for the same hospital. At last, I could see a large building ahead, but crowds had already gathered outside. As we came nearer, I saw lots of people lying on simple stretchers, badly injured, but most people were able to stand or sit as they waited for treatment for less serious injuries.

We all seemed to have something in common, though. Apart from getting treatment, everyone had come there to find someone.

'Maddy?'

I whipped round and threw myself into his arms. It was Dad!

FIVE

For a long time, Dad and I stood in a bear hug, my left arm hanging at my side. Then Dad gently pushed me away from him, his hands on my shoulders.

'Have you seen your mum?' he asked, his voice trembling.

I shook my head and winced as the pain shot up my arm. Then I realised James and

Cathy were still standing close by. I stepped back from Dad and turned to them.

'This is my dad,' I said.

Cathy smiled. 'I'm glad you've found each other, Madeleine,' she said. 'We'll be off then … You'd better get that arm fixed.'

James gave a little wave and they turned away to join a queue.

'Thanks,' Dad called after them. 'Thank you for looking after my daughter.' Then he gently inspected my arm and frowned. 'This looks bad. What happened to you?'

Through tears, I told him about being on the beach and seeing the wave coming.

'I ran back to our chalet to warn you,' I said. 'But you weren't there.'

'No … if you remember we were at Babs and Tony's chalet,' said Dad. His voice was dull and lifeless. 'We heard the roar, but didn't know what it was so we did nothing

… then slam! It took us completely by surprise.'

'The table saved me,' I said. 'I'm sure I would have drowned if I hadn't clung onto it.'

'Tony's dead.'

I gasped.

'I've just seen him … a massive blow to his head. There's a makeshift mortuary out the back of the hospital. It's full to bursting already and they're bringing more bodies in by the minute.'

I felt sick. Tony? How terrible! I had called him a middle-aged loser. He wasn't that bad. Now he was dead!

'And the hospital wards are full, too,' Dad went on. 'I've been in there looking for you all.'

'Mum? Damian?'

Dad shook his head. 'Not yet.' His eyes filled with tears. 'Thank God I've found you, Maddy.'

No one spoke to us. They just stood or sat in line, their faces pale and their eyes sad, waiting in the heat of the sun.

A helicopter buzzed overhead. Everyone shaded their eyes and watched it hovering. A side door opened and a large package was dropped out. Some people raced over to the package, but I didn't have the energy and I'm pretty sure Dad didn't either.

We asked around and hunted everywhere for Mum and Damian. In the end, we joined a long queue to see a doctor. My arm had to be set. It was very swollen and bent in all the wrong places. And it was killing me! Someone came round with bottles of water. I guzzled mine down, but it didn't make me feel any better.

'There's only two doctors on duty,' someone told us. 'More are being air-lifted in.'

We sat on the dry earth in the blazing sun, fanning ourselves with anything we could find. More bottles of water miraculously appeared to keep us alive. From time to time, Dad went off searching while I kept our place in the queue.

Each time he returned, his face seemed greyer. His shoulders sagged, he looked ten years older. More and more people were flocking to the hospital, but Mum and Damian were not among them.

At last my turn came. Dad and I followed a young nurse past rows of people on beds, trolleys, stretchers or even on the hard floor, and into a small cubicle.

'Wait here,' she said.

A few minutes later, a man took a photo of me.

'We're taking everyone's photos,' he said.

'We'll post them outside so that people can see who is here.'

Then I was examined by a young doctor. She had dark rings round her eyes and she looked really stressed. I screamed as she poked and pulled at my arm.

'First we must do X-rays,' she said. 'I believe this is badly broken. You will need to be asleep when it is set.'

I nodded. It didn't seem that important. I just wanted Mum to be there with me.

'You haven't seen my mum, have you?' I asked. 'She looks a bit like me only she's taller and a bit darker haired … '

The doctor shrugged her shoulders and shook her head.

'Sorry,' she said.

I fought back my tears. I realised what a stupid question it must seem, but I wanted to know.

'Can't anyone tell me where she is?'

'There's another hospital a few miles away,' said a nurse. 'Maybe your mum's been taken there.'

'And my brother, Damian,' I said. 'We don't know where he is, either.'

'Sorry.' The nurse shook her head then left us.

Dad and I didn't say what I guess was in both our minds – a question I had already asked myself hundreds of times. What had happened to Damian when the sea had been sucked away, then crashed back onto the shore?

At last, my turn came for the operating theatre. Dad hugged me tightly before they took me down.

'I'm going to the other hospital while you're asleep,' he said. He was trying to smile at me, but his eyes were so sad.

'I wish I hadn't said those things to Mum,' I said. 'I don't hate her.'

'I know,' he said as he turned to go.

When I came to, I was aware of being in a very crowded noisy place. I opened my eyes. Dad was sitting on the floor beside my makeshift bed, holding my right hand. My left arm was in plaster from my shoulder to my hand. It still hurt like mad.

'Hi, little sis!'

'Damian?' I whispered.

I turned my head. Damian was still wearing his wet suit, which was hanging off him in ripped shreds. His face was pale underneath his tan. But he was alive!

SIX

'I can't believe … how lucky I was,' said Damian, sitting down beside Dad. 'It was … terrifying.'

He kept pausing in the middle of sentences, as if he was having difficulty breathing.

'We'd been under the water … for quite a while … but suddenly … the fish … went crazy.'

He closed his eyes.

'They must have sensed … it was coming,' he said. 'Then it went dark … and … the sea was … I don't know … like a washing machine, I guess … We were being thrown around … in the pitch darkness … I grabbed hold … of the coral … ripped my hands to pieces.'

He opened his eyes and showed me his hands. There were deep red gashes all over his palms and fingers. I winced. They looked very sore.

'Then the sea … snatched me away … but I managed to cling … to one of my mates … a rock … more coral … and hung on … The sea was trying to … drag us away … It was ages before … we dared come up … to the surface … '

He paused and swallowed hard. 'Can't

believe what I've seen … bodies everywhere … in the sea … on the beach … inland … It's horrible.'

He suddenly burst into tears. I'd never seen Damian cry before, well, not for years, since we were kids, and it shocked me.

'We've got to … find Mum,' he cried.

Dad put his arm round him.

'I found Damian wandering round the other hospital,' he said.

'I got taken there … in a truck,' said Damian. 'But I didn't even … get to see a nurse … let alone a doctor. They were all … concentrating on the … really bad cases. Oh, Maddy … I'm so relieved you're OK.'

Dad looked at me. 'How are you feeling now, Maddy?'

I didn't really know how I felt.

'Numb,' I said. 'Apart from my arm.'

It hurt like a pneumatic drill was boring into it.

'The doctors need the bed,' said Dad. 'They want us to leave as soon as you feel OK.'

I sat bolt upright, then wished I hadn't. I clung onto Dad until the waves of dizziness and nausea had gone.

After a few minutes, I felt stronger and managed to kneel up then get up without keeling over.

'Right,' I said. 'Let's go.'

I couldn't stand the smell of the hospital or the noise of people crying or groaning. I was so relieved to get out of there.

Dad had a soggy photo of Mum in his wallet. We posted it with thousands of others on a board outside the hospital. We wrote a label to go with it with her name and what she was wearing.

'Someone must have seen her,' I tried to convince myself. 'She'll be searching frantically for us. She must be worried sick.'

That was exactly how I was feeling about her! If only we hadn't had that row.

As we walked away from the hospital, I still felt very confused. It didn't seem real. I kept wondering if I would wake up and find I had been having a ghastly nightmare.

But time passed and I didn't wake up. It was there all round us, true, real, never going away.

It was growing dark. We were all exhausted. I wanted to just curl up and sleep, blot it all out, this everlasting nightmare, this uncertainty about Mum.

I love you, Mum, I kept thinking. Perhaps if I thought it often enough it would draw her back to us.

It's the next morning now. Still no sign of Mum. We didn't search all night. How could we in the pitch dark? But we're setting off again in a few minutes. Did I sleep? I think I must have done, fitfully, full of strange, wild dreams.

Mum was in them all, always there, but never quite within reach.

They're talking about flying us home, those of us who have survived. They want us out of the way as the rescue effort is mounting. Lots of charities have set up centres. They're bringing in food, water and blankets, tents and more medical supplies.

They're very sympathetic, but that doesn't help much.

I've refused to go.

'I'm not leaving without my mum,' I told them.

Dad and Damian feel exactly the same. She's got to be out there somewhere. We're not going to give up.

We'll find her, even if it takes forever.

Another great Shades 2.0 title –

WHAT ABOUT ME?

by Helen Orme

Here is Chapter One:

Escape

'I'm sick of you – you go on all the time!' screamed Lisa at the top of her voice.

'Shut up!' Her father turned on her. 'You keep out of this.'

He swung back to her mother.

'This is all your fault.'

Lisa's mum huddled back into the corner. She was trying to make herself as small as possible, so there was less of her to hit. She couldn't do anything to protect herself, let alone Lisa.

Her dad was drunk. Again. He was always violent when he was drunk, and since he had lost his job he was drunk more and more of the time.

'I'm off out.' He glared at Lisa. 'You! Get this mess cleared up.' He stamped off, slamming the door behind him.

Lisa looked at her mum. She would get no help from her. Mrs Davis had slumped onto the floor. She was weeping now and holding her left arm close to her body. Lisa could see new bruises on her arms and face.

'Why do you put up with him, Mum?'

'What else can I do? You know we've nowhere else to go.'

'There are places you can get help.'

It was no use. Lisa had tried so many

times before. There was no way her mum would leave. She was too frightened.

Lisa decided she'd better do as her dad said. She picked up the chair and began to mop up the spilt coffee from the floor.

'Go to bed, Mum,' she said. 'I'm going out.'

She didn't know where she was going to go, but anything was better than staying at home.

She decided to go to the amusement arcade. She hadn't much money, but at least there would be people enjoying themselves.

The arcade was quite full. She recognised a few people and went over to join a group of boys she knew from school. With them, she wouldn't have to think about anything. They were always good for a laugh.

'Hiya, Nick.'

'Hiya. How's life?'

'Yeah, great. What ya gonna do tonight, then?'

'We're off to the pub in a minute – wanna come?'

It was late when Lisa got back. She'd hoped that her dad would be in bed, but as soon as she got to the door of the flat she realised she wasn't going to be that lucky.

She could hear the screams before she got to the door. Lights were on in the nearby flats and she could see the shape of a head peering through the curtains.

She burst through the door. There must be something really wrong. Her mum didn't usually make that sort of noise.

All the lights were on. Furniture had been thrown about the room. There was blood on the carpet. A lot of blood.